Happily Ever After

LIANA BROOKS

OTHER WORKS

HEROES AND VILLAINS

Even Villains Fall In Love
Even Villains Go To The Movies
Even Villains Have Interns
Even Villains Play The Hero (books 1 – 3 omnibus)
The Polar Terror

FLEET OF MALIK

Bodies In Motion
Change of Momentum
For Every Action (forthcoming)

SHORTER WORKS

All I Want For Christmas Is A Werewolf
Fey Lights
Prime Sensations
Darkness and Good

Find other works by the author at
www.lianabrooks.com

Happily Ever After

INKLET #25

LIANA BROOKS

Inkprint PRESS
www.inkprintpress.com

Copyright © 2020 Liana Brooks

All rights reserved. No part of this book may be reproduced in any form or by any electronic or mechanical means, including information storage and retrieval systems, without permission in writing from the publisher, except by a reviewer, who may quote brief passages in a review.

This is a work of fiction. All characters, organisations and events are the author's creation, or are used fictitiously.

Print ISBN: 978-1-925825-24-4
eBook ISBN: 9781393276098

www.inkprintpress.com

National Library of Australia Cataloguing-in-Publication Data
Brooks, Liana 1982 –
Happily Ever After
38 p.
ISBN: 978-1-925825-24-4
Inkprint Press, Canberra, Australia
1. Fiction—Fantasy—Contemporary 2. Fiction—Fantasy—Dark Fantasy 3. Fiction—Fantasy—Humorous
4. Fiction—Short Stories

First Print Edition: January 2020
Cover photo © Peter Pang via Pixabay
Cover design © Inkprint Press
Interior art © Amy Laurens

HAPPILY EVER AFTER

"I HATE FAIRY TALE ENDINGS!" ROSE threw the child's coloring book into the fireplace designated for burning princess memorabilia. She stooped to pick up a sheet of stickers and waved them in her husband's face. "Look at her! Look at her! Does that look like me at all? Do I have blond hair? What kind of Nordic whore do they think I am?"

She threw the stickers back into the crackling fire and grabbed a torch from the sconce on the wall. "I. Am. Sick. Of. Happy. Endings."

"What happy ending?" Gavin asked, relaxing back in his chair at the head of the table with a cup of coffee and a newspaper ten months out of date.

"The one we're supposed to have! The one that left us here!" She let loose with a stream of invectives she wouldn't have dreamed of using a few centuries ago. Time had been a bad influence on her.

"I want to die!"

She flopped into her own ornate chair next to her husband and stared at the banquet in front of them—the same banquet they'd been eating for the last four centuries. Or was it five? She'd lost count somewhere along the line.

"You can't die," said Gavin in a mild tone. "Dying isn't living happily ever after."

"I hate happily ever after."

"We haven't happily-ever-aftered in quite some time." He looked over his mug at her with a raised eyebrow.

Rose blushed. They'd been quite happy, for a few years. But there were no children in happily ever after. No visits to friends. No improvements on the castle. No wrinkles. No lines. No death. "It wouldn't have been so bad if we'd aged," she continued more mildly. "That's what normal people do. They get wrinkles and they die and sob over each other's graves."

"Old age isn't happily ever after either." He flipped the page. "Oh, look, we missed another concert."

She glared daggers at him. "Concerts aren't happily ever after, dear," she replied sarcastically. "Neither are cell phones, hot running water, or cars."

Frustrated that Gavin wouldn't take the bait, Rose stormed off to her room. She sat down at her writing desk and took up her pen, just as she'd done every night for the past few decades. To every known bookseller and movie maker, she wrote the same plea:

Kill Beauty at the end of the movie.

Wouldn't it be dramatic and sweet if she died saving her beloved? Preferably before her beloved became that guy she couldn't stand because they didn't have anything in common but a stupid flower and some wishful thinking.

The only daughter of the widower schoolmaster was meant to be an old maid, dispensing charity and maybe entering a convent before she died. She was not meant to marry some forgotten prince of a kingdom no one had ever heard of. Deep in the bone, Rose knew it was the truth.

She looked out the window at the spiky vista of pine trees and high mountains, and considered how many people she would willingly kill to go see a beach. Swimming! Sand! Surfers! Visitors told her about such things—but nowhere in happily ever after did any author ever mention the second honeymoon, or family vacations.

Dark clouds rolled over the pass and a young woman hiked into view, accompanied by the now-familiar outline of a laptop case.

"Visitor!" Rose screamed, rushing downstairs to wait for the inevitable knock. "Gavin! Get dressed! We have a visitor!"

"You never used to complain about me going naked before," he grumbled.

"That's because you were covered in fur," she snapped back. "You aren't answering the door like that."

"I hate codpieces, they pinch!" he whined.

"Do I look like I care what they pinch?" She let the topic die there; pursuing it any further would start another castle-burning fight. It wasn't really Gavin's fault. He'd been deeply in lust when they met, not love, and princes as a rule just weren't genetically programmed to be monogamous. Was it any wonder he'd gotten bored with her? Or her with him...

The inevitable knock came.

Rose threw open the door for the slightly-surprised young lady. Maybe not so young; there was a definite pudginess around the midline and confidence in the smile that belied the first bloom of youth.

"Welcome to our castle," Rose said saccharinely.

The lady smiled back. "What a fabulous costume! That must have taken days to make. But why pink? Did they have pink in the fourteenth century?"

Rose looked down at her rose-pink gown and lied. "It was red, but the dye faded."

"Well, I guess that makes it realistic!" The girl beamed at her. "Hey, I hate to beg and all, but can I borrow your phone? My car broke down coming over the pass. I coasted as far as I could, but no dice. I just need to call a repair truck and maybe a cab, since this thing's a rental."

"We don't have a phone here," Rose said. "And our cell reception—"

"—Sucks, I know." The girl sighed and looked back down the long drive. "I know this sounds psycho, but could you maybe drive me somewhere? I just need to get over to the next town. I've got a map," she said as she started to rummage through her bag.

"We don't have a car," Rose said, her teeth gritting together. Did vampires have it this hard? "Won't you come in?" she tried.

"You don't have a car?" the girl asked as she stepped through the door, not noticing as Rose slammed it shut.

"The car's in town at the moment," Gavin lied smoothly as he walked out of the breakfast room, wearing the perfectly-tailored blue coat he'd worn the first day he'd been human again.

Rose liked the coat. It brought back fond memories of a time when she didn't know what 'happily ever after' meant.

"Okay. Um, well, do you guys mind if I hang out here? I can pay admission if you take credit card."

"No need to pay!" Gavin cut in. "Usually groups book the castle for exotic vacations, but this is our down season."

"And the boss won't let you wear jeans? Geez, what a curmudgeon."

"Indeed..." Gavin fumbled then picked up his lines again. "And what is your name?"

"Em. Actually, Emina, but everyone calls me Em." She dropped her laptop bag and looked around. "This is a gorgeous place, just like a fairy tale castle, you know?"

"We try," Rose said. She left out the bit that they were trying to forget, but to each their own. "Where are you from, Em?"

"Hmm, oh, America." She blushed. "The accent gives me away, doesn't it? I know some German but it comes out like that... This..." she said, switching languages and mangling the German terribly. *"I speak much poor."*

"Thankfully, we speak English just fine," Gavin said wryly.

"Come in," Rose insisted. "You can stay here until the car gets back."

The girl smiled. "That's so kind of you. I hate to impose. Just shove me in a corner, I can write."

"You're a writer?" Rose nearly squealed with delight. "Really? You write books?"

"Um, yes? Is... is that wrong?" The girl looked to Gavin in confusion.

Gavin shook his head. "No. We like writers." He smiled, showing his teeth, but the girl didn't pick up the threat. "What do you write?"

"Horror, mostly. And some urban fantasy."

Rose considered that. Well, it wasn't perfect, but hopefully she'd finally get to die.

It took two years for the book to get published. Rose loved the red rose dripping blood on the black cover. She flipped through and laughed at the dialog on page two-fifty-one. Sauntering down to the dungeon, kicking aside the remains of some forgotten bride who had rented the castle back in the forties, she called out for their friend. "Are you down here, Em?"

A whimper, and then, "Yes."

Rose flashed her teeth in a smile. "I've been reading the book."

"And?" Em scuttled to the back of her dungeon cell.

Rose flipped open the book to page two-fifty-one and read, "Help me! The crazy princess has me chained in the basement! Somebody rescue me! I'm off route seven! In the big castle! Bring guns!" Rose looked up at Emina and tsked. "You aren't chained, dear. I would never chain you. And you can't complain about the food."

"Wedding cake for two years?" Em sobbed. "I hate wedding cake!"

Rose slammed the book shut. "Try eating it for a few centuries!"

The wooden door upstairs shattered. Commandos dressed in black stormed down the stairs.

"No!" Rose shrieked. "No! Em, stop it! Change the book!"

She couldn't really blame her for trying, but she couldn't let another woman be trapped by the power of happily ever after.

"You don't want this kind of ending!" She cried. "Save yourself!" Bullets ploughed into her side and she fell to the ground.

Em smirked and pulled a hidden chapter from under her straw mat.

A ruggedly handsome hero stepped into her cell. "All ready, Ma'am?"

Smiling, she accepted the hero's hand and got to her feet. "Cross-genre epilogue, bitch," she said as she stepped over the body of the demon princess. "The author always wins."

THE MAKING OF *HAPPILY EVER AFTER*

Once upon a time, many, many years ago, there was a group of lovely authors who called themselves the Slackers because they weren't.

Several were parents. Some were students. They all had busy lives running charities, working multiple jobs, filming movies, and generally working their collective butts off. And sometimes—just sometimes—they conjured up a few spare minutes to write stories.

Happily Ever After was one of these stories. A story about what 'Happily Ever After' really meant in the fairy tales, and how exactly one would escape such a terrible fate.

It's far from perfect, but it made my friends laugh, and that's all I wanted.

DOWNLOAD YOUR FREE EBOOK

When you buy a print book from Inkprint Press, we like to say THANK YOU by offering you the ebook for free!

Please head to www.inkprintpress.com/inklets/25/ and the use the coupon INK25LET to get your copy of this Inklet in epub AND mobi today!
(Coupon will only work once.)

Read more by Liana Brooks!

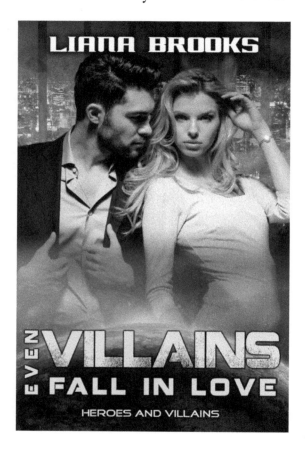

EVEN VILLAINS FALL IN LOVE

CHAPTER ONE

I knew from the first time I saw my wife that I wanted her naked. Of course, seven minutes later I wanted revenge. It wasn't that she had handed me my first defeat or ruined my chances for world domination that year, it was the way she kissed me good-bye. She sent my head spinning, then walked away as if I were the least important person in the world.

Once my arm healed, I stole some new equipment, cloned some new minions, and I felt a little different.

I wanted revenge, with a side order of naked.

ACROSS THE DINNER table, Tabitha devoured him with dark, ocean-blue eyes. She put a bite of lettuce in her mouth, full lips pursing around it. Eating salad never looked so good. Her tongue darted out to lick away a stray drop of dressing. She winked at him, promising with every move to do the same to him. "It's almost bedtime," she said, her voice husky and luscious.

"I don't wanna go to bed!" one of the quads screamed.

"What about cake? Don't we get birthday cake?" another asked.

Evan winked back at his wife from the far side of the table, separated by a few feet and four precocious just-turned-five-year olds, all as stunning as their mother with big, round eyes and hair that fell in loose curls meant to trap hairbrushes and sticky substances.

He had to peek at the eyes to see who was talking. Maria had green eyes, Angela's eyes were blue like Tabitha's, Delilah's eyes were brown like his, and Blessing—their stillborn who miraculously survived—had purple eyes. The waif in question had blue eyes.

"Angela," Evan said, "after dinner it's pajama time, and then story time."

"Mommy doesn't have a bedtime!" Angela wailed.

Tabitha winked at him again. "Tell you what, tonight Mommy will go to bed the same time you do. Right after we eat cake." She leaned over to give Angela a hug.

All Evan could see was the deep V plunge of her tight blue shirt. Oh, yeah. Crime didn't always pay, but altering someone's moral compass sure put the O's back in the bedroom.

The cake was split into fourths, equal parts purple, white, green, and blue so each girl could have her favorite color in the cake.

Baking four cakes was unreasonable; there weren't any grandparents left to celebrate with, and neighbors had an annoying habit of asking uncomfortable questions. Saying little things like, "You look just like Doctor Charm! Do you remember him? Whatever happened to that guy? Do you know how hard it is to put together a good Villains vs. Heroes fantasy league without him?" made for awkward evenings.

So they had a quiet family party. Cake, then presents, after which he hurried the girls off to bed so he could read Dilly Duck's ABCs in record time before rushing to the bedroom, hoping to catch Tabitha still in the shower.

She was already out and wearing a blue satin robe that caressed her skin in exactly the way he wanted to. Rose-scented candles cast sensuous shadows on the walls.

Tabitha turned, lips curved in an inviting smile. Long fingers twined with the sash of her robe. She tossed her honey-blonde hair in the way she always did when she was about to argue, posing with feet apart and one hand casually resting on her waist. "Sweetie, we need to talk."

Evan wiped grease-stained hands on his jeans as he forced a smile. "Sure, babes, anything you want."

"Really?" She slunk forward, all sinewy limbs and doe eyes. "Promise?" Tabitha nuzzled his nose. One hand flirted up the back of his neck to play with his hair. The other traveled downward, right to his zipper.

Oh, yes, the little Morality Machine in the basement was working just fine. Another thirty, maybe forty years of this and he'd consider retiring.

Or turning the machine down so his wife wasn't quite a sex kitten every day of the week.

Maybe only days with Y in them.

"Sweetie?" She nibbled his ear. "I want to go back to work."

"What?" Evan actually pushed himself away from her, something he wasn't sure was possible in any other circumstance.

Tabitha tucked her chin and pouted.

"Tabby-cat, I love you, but work? I've got my... stuff... in the lab. I'm busy. And we can't afford daycare for the girls. We're barely making ends meet as it is. Do you really want to go back to being Zephyr Girl? Crime fighting is a game for the young, baby. You're not nineteen anymore."

"I'm twenty-nine. A very"—her hips pressed against his tight jeans just so—"very healthy twenty-nine."

He shivered at her touch. "You're cheating."

"I want to do this, Evan." She ground against the thick denim.

"You can do me all you want, baby."

She stepped back, frowning. "I'm serious."

"So am I." Evan sighed, reaching for his wife. "Sweetie, I love you, but what's the point in being a superhero?

The government stipend barely covers the dry-cleaning bill. If it's money you want, write another tell-all superhero book. The Spanish Mask sold his third last month."

Tabitha crossed her arms. "I don't want to write another book just for royalties while you're between jobs."

He waved a finger at her. "I'm not between jobs. I work freelance in the computer business. I'm self-employed. That's not the same as being between jobs."

"Between paychecks then."

"We will have a solid income. This project I'm working on, Tabby-cat, it's going to set us up for life. We're never going to worry about money again. I promise. Give me a couple of weeks and everything is going to be perfect." He caught her hand and pulled her into his arms. The faint scent of her spicy perfume left him dizzy with need.

She rested her head on his chest. "I

want to save the world. Have you seen the news, Evan? An entire town in Kansas held hostage for a week by a bomb scare before a superhero was able to get in to defuse the situation. A week! I could have that done between grocery shopping and paying the bills. Ten minutes, no pulling punches."

"I know, baby. No one is better at this stuff than you. But I need you at home, Tabby. Having you out there scares me. I'm terrified I'd lose you. Why don't you wait until I finish this project? I'll be done by the time the election rolls around. Two more weeks. Once I get paid we'll look at this again. I have that armor design for you, I just need some time to put it together."

Tabitha sighed. "You've been saying that since we got married."

"Well, my nights are busy." He nibbled her ear as he tugged her sash loose. "Are you complaining?"

Tabitha stretched against him, sending a delightful frisson of lust up his spine. "I thought you gave up the super villain schemes."

He twitched. "I did, baby. Of course I did."

"But you're keeping me here. Isn't that a little selfish? Just a teeny-tiny bit super villain-ish?" She slipped her hand between his pants and his skin.

"Ah!" He caught her hand so he could think clearly. "Not selfish. Necessary. Like oxygen or sex."

"Don't you mean water?"

"No, definitely sex." Evan slid her robe off and tossed it into a corner. "Come here, Tabby-cat, I'll make you purr."

She tugged at his shirt, pulling it up. The shirt joined the robe on the other side of the room. "What are you doing down in that lab?" she asked as her hands drew lazy circles on his back.

Ten seconds, that's all he'd need to

get her panties off. Three more to drop his pants. "What was the question?"

"What are you doing in the lab? What's this project?"

"Oh, computer stuff. I told you. To help tally everything on election night. I'm trying to make the process run smoother so we don't have to worry about recounts."

"Hmmm." She gave him a dubious frown.

Tabitha was built like a supermodel and had a superhero name straight from Campy Comics, but her brain was Mensa all the way. "And this computer program has nothing to do with world domination, or get-rich-quick schemes?"

Evan contrived to look wounded. "Tabby-cat, how can you ask that?"

"Because you spent ten years as a villainous criminal mastermind?"

"I wasn't a mastermind, I was a super villain, there's a difference. Masterminds are just thugs with money. My crimes had artistic flare. I was practically Robin Hood! Robbing from the rich and scandalous, and giving to me."

"Robin Hood gave to the poor," Tabitha said with a laugh. "You were never poor."

He caught her hand, pulling her close. "Poor is relative. Besides, I'm reformed now. You showed me the error of my wicked ways. Although"—he leaned in for a kiss—"if you'd like to remind me why I gave up a lucrative life of crime, I have the evening free."

Keep reading! Head to
lianabrooks.com/books/
heroesandvillains/even-villains-
fall-in-love/
to buy your copy now!

ABOUT THE AUTHOR

LIANA BROOKS absolutely does *not* live in a Transylvanian castle overlooking a steep cliff where the bones of unwary travellers have an uneasy rest and haunt the living. She much prefers living near a beach and making friends, not enemies.

Brooks writes the popular *Fleet of Malik* series of connected sci-fi romances about re-building after a decades long war and has a cult-following for her *Heroes and Villains* series of superhero romances.

You can find out more about Liana at her website, www.lianabrooks.com.

INKLETS

Collect them all! Released on the 1st and 15th of each month.

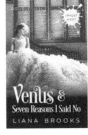

Milton Keynes UK
Ingram Content Group UK Ltd.
UKHW041856290124
436916UK00001B/1